The Fragile Force

D0465404

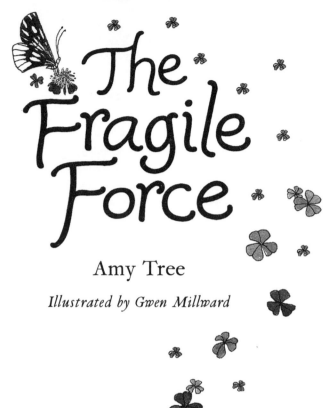

The Fragile Force

Amy Tree

Illustrated by Gwen Millward

Orion
Children's Books

First published in Great Britain in 2008
by Orion Children's Books
a division of the Orion Publishing Group Ltd
Orion House
5 Upper St Martin's Lane
London WC2H 9EA
An Hachette Livre UK Company

1 3 5 7 9 8 6 4 2

A catalogue record for this book is
available from the British Library.

ISBN 978 1 84255 654 2

Printed in Great Britian by Mackays of Chatham

Fashion Jewellery included:
Not suitable for children under 36 months.
Contains small parts which can be dangerous if swallowed.

www.orionbooks.co.uk
www.charmseekers.co.uk

For Mark, Bridget, Ghiselle and Isadora
With love — A.T.

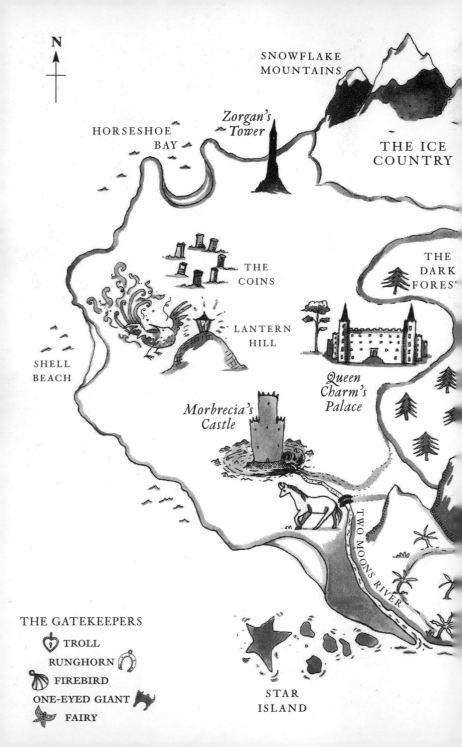

KARISMA

CAPE
CAT

CLOVER FIELDS

HEARTMOOR

DOLPHIN BAY

MOUNT
FORTUNA

The Silver Pool

KEY
POINT

SWAMPS

JUNGLE

MERMAID
ROCK

BUTTERFLY BAY

The Thirteen Charms of Karisma

When Charm became queen of Karisma, the wise
and beautiful Silversmith made her a precious gift.
It was a bracelet. On it were fastened thirteen silver
amulets, which the Silversmith called "charms",
in honour of the new queen.

It was part of Karisma law. Whenever there
was a new ruler the Silversmith made a special gift,
to help them care for the world they had inherited.
And this time it was a bracelet. She told Queen
Charm it was magical because the charms held
the power to control the forces of nature and
keep everything in balance. She must take the
greatest care of them. As long as she, and she
alone, had possession of the charms all would be
well.

And so it was, until the bracelet was stolen by
a spider, and fell into the hands of Zorgan, the
magician. Then there was chaos!

One

A gust of cold wind blows through an open window in the Silversmith's workshop. Caught in the current is a golden butterfly; the delicate insect flutters dangerously near some candles, brightly burning in a row . . .

"Oh!" gasps the Silversmith, rushing to save it from the flickering flames. Gently she cups the fragile butterfly in her hands, then exclaims with delight: "A Golden Ringlet.* How pretty!"

✶ ✶

* **Golden Ringlet** – a butterfly native to Karisma, this species feeds on clover nectar

3

Sensing it has found a safe place to rest, the exhausted butterfly settles. Now the Silversmith looks more closely at the intricate patterns on its wings, and marvels at its beauty.

"*Spider web and butterfly – hidden strength in small things lie,*" she tells the butterfly.

Another icy draught rattles the window-latch. A look of sorrow falls, like an evening shadow, across the Silversmith's lovely face. She reflects how, since the magical charms have been lost, the winds have changed; the warm winds of the south have whipped themselves into a frenzy of freezing gales. She knows the Golden Ringlets are powerless to fly against these raging storms and rain. It is for this very reason they haven't migrated to the clover fields, even though Karisman farmers depend on them to pollinate their crops. A good harvest means plenty of flour to make clover-bread – enough to feed everyone in the land. But poor crops this year have resulted in hardship and famine; and the butterflies are hungry too, starved of the sweet clover nectar they need. It is a terrible state of affairs!

She looks at the thirteen magic candles; nine still burn – nine beacons glowing for their missing charms – and she thinks of her Charmseeker, Sesame Brown. Ah, Sesame! Already she's shown such courage in finding four of the precious charms – the heart, the horseshoe, the shell and the cat. The Silversmith fears more dangers lie ahead, but she knows Sesame won't give up until she's found every charm.

She crosses to the window.

"Sesame *will* find them," she whispers to the butterfly, before she sets it free. "Then all will be well, you'll see!"

And with a flutter of golden wings, it flies away.

Two

"Oh, well done Sesame!" said Jodie. "That was perfect."

It was a Saturday morning and attractive riding instructor, Jodie Luck, was teaching Sesame to jump.

"Yep. Great stuff, Ses!" shouted Nic, re-running a sequence of pictures on his camcorder.

He'd stayed to watch Sesame's lesson, instead of rushing off to work as usual. Sesame was riding her favourite pony, Silver, and had cleared three jumps in a row. She cantered once around the school, before bringing Silver gently to a halt.

"You're the best pony in the world!" she said, patting his neck.

"And you have the makings of a good rider," said Jodie, smiling at Sesame. "You were brilliant today."

Sesame smiled; she was pleased she'd ridden well in front of her dad. Lesson over, she walked Silver back to the stables, while Jodie and Nic followed on behind, chatting.

"I think Sesame's ready to enter a gymkhana," said Jodie. "She's great with Silver. They're made for each other."

"All due to your expert tuition!" said Nic, seizing the opportunity to pay Jodie a compliment.

The two had met briefly twice before and Nic had been looking forward to seeing Jodie again. Since Sesame's mum had died, Nic had divided his time between bringing up Sesame and working hard as a press photographer. Somehow he hadn't found time (or, maybe he hadn't *made* time) to think about anyone else – until now. Jodie was different, and he wanted to make a good impression.

Walking across the busy yard, Nic couldn't help looking at Jodie; he liked the way the colour of her shirt matched her soft blue eyes. In fact, Nic was so distracted he didn't notice a wheelbarrow parked in his way . . .

"WHOOPS!" he exclaimed, crashing into the barrow. It tipped over and he fell headfirst into a load of mucky bedding.

"Nic!" cried Jodie.

The sudden commotion spooked Silver. Sesame brought him under control and soothed him. When she looked round to see what had happened, there was her dad spread-eagled in the straw.

"Argh! I don't believe it," she said, under her breath. "Dad, you're sooo embarrassing!"

But Sesame couldn't help feeling sorry for him. She knew how foolish he must feel in front of everyone – especially Jodie! To make matters worse, a girl called Olivia Pike was standing there, sniggering. Sesame knew Olivia from school; she kept her dappled-grey mare, Misty Morning, at Jodie's yard, and was always bragging about owning her own pony. Sesame thought she was a spoilt little brat and they were definitely *not* the best of friends! To add to her dismay, Sesame noticed that the wheelbarrow had Olivia's name painted on the side.

"Oh dear," said Olivia, obviously enjoying Sesame's discomfort. "Look what your dad's done."

Sesame glared at her, but concentrated on calming Silver. Jodie gave Olivia a sharp look, before turning her attention to Nic.

"You okay?" she said, offering him her hand. "Here, let me help you."

"I'm fine!" said Nic, struggling to his feet. He wished the ground would swallow him up.

"Come and have a coffee," said Jodie, tactfully removing a piece of straw from his collar. She looked across at Sesame and smiled. "Untack Silver and give him a good rub down," she said. "Then come and join us."

"Thanks," said Sesame, and led Silver into his stable.

Olivia looked mad, but Jodie simply said, "Clear up this mess please, Olivia. Another time, don't leave your barrow where people can fall over it!"

Three

"Dork! What are you doing?" snarled Morbrecia. Queen Charm's most trusted officer was taken completely by surprise.

"N-n-n-nothing!" spluttered Dork. "I was, um, just passing. Nice day for a walk . . ."

"What? Dressed like a bush!" snapped Morbrecia. "Don't give me that. You were SPYING on me. I suppose my charming little sister sent you?"

It was true. Dork *was* carrying out Charm's orders by keeping an eye on Morbrecia. The queen had told him to report anything that would prove her sister was after the missing charms. Dork had camouflaged himself with leaves (not very successfully) and was hiding, when Morbrecia crept up on him. Dork's disguise was starting to wilt, and so was his courage — Morbrecia looked furious.

"P-p-probably some misunderstanding, Your Royal Highness," said Dork, valiantly trying to reason with her. "You were, er, seen chasing two Charmseekers through Lantern Hill. Agapogo Day.✶ Remember?"

Morbrecia remembered very well. Those balam✶✶ Outworlders✶✶✶ had just got away with *another* charm — the exquisite little shell. She'd so *nearly* caught them too! As it was, all she'd managed to grab was Sesame's flip-flop. The memories whizzed through her head, and Morbrecia thought of a way to spin them to her advantage . . .

✶ ✶

✶ **Agapogo Day** – a holiday in honour of Agapogo, the dragon of the Silver Pool.
✶ ✶ **Balam** – cursed, an angry exclamation
✶ ✶ ✶ **Outworlders** – the name Karismans call people from our world

"Me? Chasing them?" she protested. "I'm a princess, why would I be chasing them?"

Dork gulped.

"Well, I was informed . . . that is, Her Majesty *thinks* you may have wanted to keep the charm for yourself—"

Morbrecia pretended to look offended.

"Don't you think that *if* I had been chasing them, it was because I wanted to return the charm to my sister, you magwort!"* she yelled. "I've seen Sesame and her friend snooping round here before. I tell you, *they're* stealing the charms and taking them back to the Outworld."

* *

*Magwort — probably the worst name you could call anyone! General term for a fool

Dork looked confused. Was Sesame taking the charms back to the Outworld? How awful. He was sure Charm didn't know that. Who should he believe? He was beginning to think Morbrecia had been wrongly accused – at least, he would like to think so.

"I remember meeting Sesame Brown in the Dark Forest," he recalled. "It was the day after the queen's bracelet was stolen. She was helping a tunganora* find its mother – that's what she *said* she was doing. When I mentioned the bracelet, she seemed really keen to find it. Come to think of it, her very words were, 'Sesame Brown will track it down!'"

"There you are!" cried Morbrecia triumphantly. "What more proof do you need? You should be after those Charmseekers, not me. Now clear off and leave me alone!"

Dork made his way back to the palace, through the Dark Forest. As he walked along, several thoughts churned messily inside his head. He needed to sort them out, so he jotted everything down in his notebook:

* *

*Tunganora – a small ape-like animal with long, pink shaggy hair, found only in Karisma

1. I am in a tricky situation!
2. My orders are to spy on Morbrecia.
3. Morbrecia thinks I should be watching the Charmseekers – and she could be right!
4. My tummy's rumbling, so it must be nearly lunchtime.
5. Will decide what to do about
   (a) Morbrecia and
   (b) Charmseekers after lunch . . .

As Dork wrote the word "lunch", he thought he detected a whiff of fish, wafting through the trees. The smell of food made his stomach rumble like thunder, and he hurried on his way.

Four

On Monday morning Lossy, Sesame's grandmother, drove her to school early. Sesame's class were learning about rainforests, and today Mrs Wilks was taking them to visit the Natural History Museum in London, to help them with their project work. She had told everyone to assemble in the playground in good time. "The coach leaves at nine o'clock sharp," she'd warned them.

Lossy kissed Sesame goodbye at the gates. "Have a great time," she said. "Mind those dinosaurs don't eat your lunch!"

Sesame laughed. "We're going to a *butterfly* exhibition, Gran," she said.

Walking across the playground, Sesame looked out for her best friend Maddy, and hoped she wouldn't be late. She spotted Olivia Pike and her cronies, and they spotted her. They started laughing. Oh great! thought Sesame. I bet Olivia has told them about Dad tripping over at the stables. Then she heard voices calling her.

"Ses! Over here."

It was Gemma Green and Liz Robinson. Relieved to see them, Sesame waved and ran over. After they'd hugged, Gemma said: "We must all sit together on the coach."

"As far as possible from *her*!" added Liz, tossing a look in Olivia's direction. "She's a pain."

"Yeah," agreed Sesame, absent-mindedly. She was worried about Maddy and wished she would hurry up. She pulled out her mobile and texted:

WHERE R U?
COACH LEAVES
SKL AT 9! SES.
MWAH MWAH

Maddy replied straightaway:

FORGOT PACKED
LUNCH. MUM MAD COS
WE R STUCK IN TRAFFIC.
MY FAULT! CU SOON.
DNT
GO WITHOUT ME! LOL

Sesame sighed. It was typical of Maddy to forget something! Just then Mrs Wilks appeared, holding a clipboard.

"Are we all here?" She called out everyone's name on her list. They were all there – except Maddy Webb.

"No Maddy?" queried Mrs Wilks.

"She's coming," said Sesame quickly. "I've just had a text. She'll be here any minute!"

"Well, it's time to board the coach," said Mrs Wilks. "If Maddy's not here by nine, I'm afraid we'll have to leave without her."

"Oh, *what* a shame," said Olivia, within Sesame's earshot. "Sesame's bestie will miss all the fun!"

Sesame ignored her. She sat with Gemma and Liz on the coach and saved a seat for Maddy. Mrs Wilks walked up and down the aisle counting everyone. Then she looked at her watch. One minute to nine! Sesame's heart was pounding. Oh Maddy, hurry up, hurry up! she thought. She peered anxiously through the window, as the coach driver turned the key in the ignition . . . Suddenly Sesame gave a shout:

"MADDY!"

Everyone turned round. There was Maddy pelting along the pavement, her backpack flying. She scrambled up the steps of the coach, panting. Mrs Wilks sighed with relief.

"Just in time!" she said. "Now, hurry up and find a seat."

"Here!" cried Sesame, her eyes shining with delight.

As Maddy plonked down next to her, Sesame had the satisfaction of seeing the look of disappointment on Olivia's face. Maddy had made it, after all.

The journey to London sped by. Sesame, Maddy, Gemma and Liz spent a while catching up on all the gossip. Then Sesame confided in Maddy about her dad's friendship with Jodie Luck.

"They really like each other," she said quietly.

"Jodie's cool," said Maddy, chewing a jellybean. "For a grown-up, that is."

Sesame smiled. She knew what Maddy meant.

"Are they all lovey 'n' stuff?" Maddy asked, as she offered Sesame a sweet. "Have they *kissed* yet?"

"No!" retorted Sesame. Then she added more cautiously, "Well, I don't *think* so."

Sesame wouldn't have minded even if her dad and Jodie *had* kissed — but she didn't want the whole class to know! So she quickly changed the subject. Sitting behind them were Gemma and Liz. Liz usually had her nose in a book, and she was reading one now. It was an exciting story, set in a jungle. Gemma happened to glance at a picture on the page.

"Oh, look Ses," she said, without thinking. "It looks like that bird we saw in Karisma—"

Sesame was taken completely by surprise. She rounded furiously on Gemma.

"Sssssh!" she hissed.

"Sorry," mumbled Gemma, turning red. "I forgot."

Too late! Liz was curious to know more.

"What bird?" she asked. "Where's Karisma? What *are* you talking about?"

Maddy glared at Gemma, and Sesame said the first thing that came into her head:

"Um – something we saw on TV," she fibbed. "Tell you about it later."

Liz wasn't convinced.

"That's so not true, Ses. I *know* you're keeping something from me. You'd better tell me later."

Feeling a bit left out, Liz went back to her book and the others spent the rest of the journey remembering their adventure in Karisma.

There was so much to see and do at the Natural History Museum. Mrs Wilks had arranged to visit the Amazing Butterflies exhibition, so that's where they went first. On the way they passed the skeleton of an enormous dinosaur, and Sesame couldn't resist stopping to take a closer look.

"Diplodocus," she announced, reading the inscription. "One hundred and fifty million years old."

"Phew!" said Maddy.

"Cool," said Gemma.

"A monster!" said Liz.

After the awkward situation on the coach, Sesame had tried her best to make Liz feel included. She didn't want to hurt her feelings, but she couldn't explain about Karisma — yet. Liz had cheered up, determined not to let anything spoil her day. She

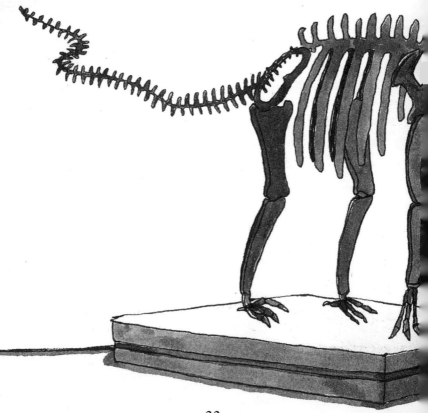

stood happily with the others gawping at the dinosaur, until she noticed the rest of the class striding away in the distance.

"Quick," she said. "We'd better catch up."

So Sesame, Maddy, Gemma and Liz were at the end of the queue when they eventually stepped inside the tropical butterfly house. They all gasped. It was hot and steamy – just like a jungle – with

palms and fruit trees and butterflies everywhere, flitting between exotic plants with brightly coloured flowers. Almost immediately, a yellow butterfly settled on Sesame's hand.

"Fabulous!" she exclaimed, examining the pretty patterns on its wings.

"There's one on a lemon tree," cried Maddy. "And another over there."

Gemma and Liz tried to identify some of them from pictures on a card. "Green longwing? Blue peacock? Scarlet swallowtail . . ." they read aloud.

But Sesame wasn't listening. Suddenly she felt light-headed. Perhaps it was the heat? She pressed her hand to her forehead. Something strange was happening, because she had the weirdest feeling she was growing smaller. Was she shrinking or were the butterflies getting bigger? Sesame looked up. All around her were shimmering golden wings, and she felt herself floating upwards . . .

She was vaguely aware of Maddy, Gemma and Liz, their urgent voices echoing eerily inside her head,

"Ses. Ses. Ses . . . "

Then all four of them were drifting, light as feathers, up, up, up into a clear blue sky. Now Sesame *knew* what was happening. Somehow they'd stumbled across a way into that other world she'd discovered. Karisma. Yes, that was it! Sesame prickled with excitement and wondered what lay in store for them this time.

Five

The girls flew through the air. They were guided by butterflies, whose golden wings fluttered in the breeze like windblown kites. They drifted over a sparkling sea, before gliding down to Butterfly Bay, a stretch of pure white sand on the edge of a jungle.

Pogg, the fairy, saw them land. Like all gatekeepers, she had strict orders to stay alert for the return of the Charmseekers. If they happened to come through her gate, she was to inform Queen Charm without delay. Could these be them? Pogg wondered, as she went to greet them.

"Fairday,"* she said. "I'm Pogg. Welcome to Karisma!"

Sesame smiled at the fairy. She was thrilled to be back.

* *

Fairday — a typical Karisman friendly greeting

"I'm Sesame Brown," she said, and at once Pogg recognised her name. She *was* a Charmseeker! When Maddy, Gemma and Liz got to their feet, Sesame introduced them, too.

"*Four* Charmseekers?" enquired Pogg.

"Yes," said Maddy, proudly. "That's us!"

Liz was trying hard to take everything in. She looked helplessly from Pogg to Maddy.

"Charmseekers? What are *they*?" she whispered.

"Tell you later," said Maddy.

"Yes, *promise*," added Sesame, remembering what she'd said on the coach.

Pogg wrote a message on a scroll, and while she was doing that the girls noticed there were golden butterflies everywhere, settling in the trees and flitting around them — just like the ones at the exhibition. When Pogg had finished, she rolled up the scroll and blew three short blasts on a whistle. Another fairy appeared from nowhere, smartly dressed in a red and gold uniform, with a mailbag over her shoulder. She was a royal messenger.

"Take this to Queen Charm," said Pogg, handing her the scroll. "Her Majesty will be pleased to know four Charmseekers have just arrived!"

After the messenger had gone, the girls spent a few minutes talking to Pogg. Sesame was curious about the golden butterflies, which had brought them.

"Golden Ringlets," said Pogg. "The poor things are hungry. They should have migrated by now, to feed on clover. But they haven't been able to this winter."

"Oh dear," said Sesame. "Why?"

"The winds have changed," explained Pogg. "Since the magical charms were stolen, everything's gone wrong. The butterflies can't fly in bad weather."

"But some of them made a *special* journey, to bring us here," observed Sesame. "They're amazing. So brave! We must find another charm. The sooner we can find them all, the better for the butterflies – and everyone."

Pogg pulled a little book from her pocket and gave it to Sesame.

"Quite right," she said. "Here. Take this. It's a story about a brave Golden Ringlet. You'll like it."

"Thank you," said Sesame, putting the book in her pocket to read later. Right now she couldn't wait to start looking for the charms.

"How long have we got?" she asked Pogg.

"You must return before Larissa✱ turns red," the gatekeeper told her, mysteriously. "And watch out for snatchworts." ✱ ✱

"Larissa? queried Liz, completely confused.

"Snatchworts?" said Gemma.

But there was no reply. Pogg had simply vanished.

"So this is Karisma!" said Liz, as the four friends set off through the jungle.

"I hope we don't meet any monsters," said Gemma, looking over her shoulder.

"We'll be too busy looking for charms to worry about them!" said Sesame cheerfully. "Nine of the thirteen are still missing."

✱ ✱

✱ **Larissa** – a group of five stars, which turn red, one by
one
✱ ✱ **Snatchwort** – a flesh-eating tropical plant

31

"What are they?" asked Liz, who knew nothing about the magical charms.

"I can remember some of them," piped up Maddy.

"There's a butterfly . . . snowflake . . . lantern . . . coin and a star—"

"—Dolphin, moon, clover and key," said Sesame, completing the list of charms yet to be found. "Sesame Brown will track them down!"

"What about the other four?" asked Liz, brushing aside a branch.

So Sesame told Liz what they were.

"I've seen them," said Gemma. "They're lovely. Ses keeps them in her jewellery box at home."

"With the silver bracelet," added Sesame. "When I've found *all* the charms, I shall return them to Her Majesty, Queen Charm of Karisma."

The Charmseekers looked around. Everything here grew so big. Twisted creepers hung above their heads, like woody ropes; thick roots straddled their path and the trees were as tall as towers. It was warm and humid in the jungle and full of buzzing, biting insects.

"Ouch!" yelped Maddy, swatting at a mosquito on her leg.

The girls made slow progress – there were so many obstacles in their way.

"I wish I was riding Silver," said Sesame, clambering over a fallen branch. "I could jump this easily—" She broke off suddenly.

"What's up?" said Maddy.

"I thought I heard something," she said.

They all stood and listened.

CROAK-RIBBIT CROAK-RIBBIT CROAK-CROAK

Hopping along the path came a whopping great toad, with bulging eyes.

"Ugh!" exclaimed Sesame.

"Mega scary!" said Maddy.

"I think I'm going to be sick," said Gemma.

But Liz was fascinated. The toad looked prehistoric – like a creature from another age. She watched as it shot out its tongue, zapped a mosquito –

shlup

– and swallowed it with a gulp. Then it hopped away along a path they hadn't noticed before.

"A hidden path!" said Liz. "Come on. Let's follow the toad and see where it goes."

Six

Dork tucked into a large portion of hog pie* and considered the situation – he had important things on his mind:

1. Was Morbrecia telling the truth?
2. Were the Charmseekers stealing the charms?
3. Should he ask Queen Charm for her advice?

After a while, he decided to discuss everything with the queen. On his way to see her, Dork met the royal messenger Pogg had sent. She took something from her bag.

"What's that?" he enquired.

* *

*Hog pie – a Karisman speciality, similar to a pork pie

"Important news for Her Majesty," said the fairy, waving the scroll. "The Charmseekers are back! Four of them have arrived at Butterfly Bay."

"I'll take it," said Dork, whipping the scroll from her hand. "I'm going there myself."

The messenger was somewhat taken aback, but she trusted Dork to carry out this task.

"Four of them," muttered Dork, when the fairy had gone. "Those girls mean business this time. So, Morbrecia was right. Sesame's gang are out to steal the charms! The situation is worse than I feared . . ."

Dork changed his mind about seeing the queen, and tucked the scroll in his pocket.

"If I tell Her Maj. about my suspicions, she'll only worry," he reasoned to himself. "Best to sort things out first and see her later."

So Dork set off to look for the Charmseekers. He didn't *like* the idea of going into the jungle – he'd heard it was dangerous. But it was his duty to save those charms, and he thought the queen would be pleased if he captured Sesame Brown. She might even give him a medal . . .

Meanwhile, in the Dark Forest, Morbrecia had arranged to meet the gribblers – Varg, Gorz and Bod. The gribblers stood about dribbling and scratching.

Morbrecia held a hanky to her nose – the stench of
rotting fish was unbearable, but she urgently needed
their help.

"Follow Dork," she ordered the gribblers. "Track
him wherever he goes. With any luck, he'll lead you
to those balam Outworlders, Sesame and—"

At the very mention of Sesame, Varg gave a strangled gasp and spat out a revolting blob of slime.

"Leave Ssheshame to ush, Princhess Morbreeesha," Varg leered. He grinned horribly, drawing back lizard lips over yellowing teeth. "We'll get her thish time, you'll sheee!"

"Good, good," said Morbrecia, nimbly avoiding a shower of slimy spray. "But remember, if Sesame finds another charm . . . bring it to ME!"

Seven

The hidden path led to a spectacular waterfall called Silver Falls. The Charmseekers had followed the toad for some time, until it had disappeared under a rock. Now they stood marvelling at the water cascading down a ravine. Clouds of silvery mist filled the air; the girls could hardly hear themselves speak above the roar of rushing water.

"Wow!" yelled Sesame and Maddy together.

"Awesome!" cried Gemma.

"I'm soaked!" shouted Liz, as she caught some spray.

She was pleased she'd taken the lead in bringing the others here – it made her feel part of the team.

They peered down at the river, far below. It was Two Moons River, and they spotted some fish leaping out of the water.

"Remind me not to fall in there," said Sesame. "Those are skreel.* They eat people! Remember we saw some before, Maddy?"

* *

*Skreel – small flesh-eating fish

Maddy nodded.

"In the lake at Morbrecia's castle."

"Who's Morbrecia?" asked Liz, sighing. "There's *so* much I don't know!"

"She's a princess," explained Sesame. "Honestly Liz, I'll tell you everything later. Right now we *have* to look for the charms."

So the four searched in the undergrowth and peered into plants with petals as big as dinner plates, until Maddy's tummy started to rumble. "It's *ages* since I had breakfast!" she complained. "Lucky we've still got our packed lunches. Let's stop for a while and have something to eat."

So everyone agreed. Sesame was just taking a bite from a peanut-butter sandwich, when the others screamed and yelled,

"SESAME! BEHIND YOU!"

Sesame turned. The sight that met her eyes made her choke. A gigantic creature, with an extraordinarily long neck and a tiny head, was peering at her.

"I th-th-think it's a dip-dip-diplodocus!" she spluttered. And dropped her sandwich.

Sesame was almost right. It was in fact a Plodopus*. Apparently this one had a particular

* * * * * * * * * * * * * * * * * * * *

*Plodopus – a plant-eating dinosaur, believed to be a close relative of Diplodocus, which lived in the Outworld millions of years ago

liking for peanut-butter and, with its keen sense of smell, had caught a whiff of Sesame's snack, wafting through the trees. The girls watched in stunned amazement, as

it stretched out its neck and snatched the fallen sandwich. After swallowing it in one gulp, it rooted around for more.

"P-p-p-please, help yourself," said Sesame, offering it the entire contents of her lunch box. The dinosaur ate the lot, gave a satisfied burp and wandered off.

"Did I just see what I thought I saw?" said Liz.

"I think so," said Gemma, blinking.

"Let's eat fast in case there's another one," said Maddy. "You can share my lunch, Ses. Mum packed loads."

"Thanks," said Sesame. "You're a star!"

They finished their lunch then packed up their bags. By this time, to their surprise, they saw it was growing dark.

"Perhaps Karisma days are shorter than ours?" suggested Liz. She looked at her watch. "It's not even lunchtime at home."

Sesame looked at her watch; its face had changed to show Karisma time. It had happened before. There were pictures of five stars — and one of them was red.

"Got it!" she exclaimed. "Remember Pogg telling us about Larissa? It must be a group of stars."

They looked up and, sure enough, there was one red star shining above — just like the one on Sesame's watch.

"Come on," said Sesame. "We've wasted enough time. We *must* find a charm and be at the gate before all the stars turn red!"

There appeared to be only one way to go. A path led down the side of the steep ravine to Two Moons River, and at one point it went under Silver Falls.

"I'm scared," shouted Gemma. She was standing on a narrow, rocky ledge facing a wall of tumbling water. The sound was deafening.

"Follow me!" shouted Sesame. "You'll be fine."

"We're right behind you," cried Maddy and Liz.

The four of them edged their way slowly under the falls . . .

The rock-face glistened. Every now and then a silvery sparkle caught Sesame's eye — and once she was *sure* she'd spotted another charm. But it was only a trick of the light, and to her disappointment they reached the other side without finding anything.

Relieved to be out in the open again, the girls ran down the path to the river. Away in the distance, Sesame spotted a castle, which looked vaguely familiar.

"Look, Maddy," she said. "Isn't that Morbrecia's castle?"

"Yeah, I think you're right," said Maddy. "Remember we got chased across her lake by those horrid . . . what were they called?"

"Gribblers!" said Sesame, and shuddered at the thought of them.

As she said it, a gust of wind blew in their direction, and suddenly the air was filled with the smell of rotting FISH.

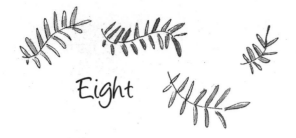

Eight

Dork took the quickest route to the jungle, passing Morbrecia's castle on the way. He regretted eating such a large piece of hog pie for lunch, because now he was feeling sleepy. Reaching Two Moons River, he found a quiet spot on the riverbank and sat down to rest.

"I'll just have a quick nap," he said to himself. "Then I'll get after Sesame Brown!"

As it happened, Varg, Gorz and Bod were not far behind. They had been cunning enough to keep downwind of Dork, so he wouldn't smell them as they followed in his tracks. But when they got to the riverbank, the wind blew a fishy stink towards him – only by this time Dork was asleep and didn't notice. Then the gribblers caught sight of the Charmseekers.

"There," said Varg gleefully. "Dork has lead ush to Ssheshame, jush like Morbreeesha said he would!"

At that precise moment Sesame saw the gribblers.

"RUN!" she shouted to the others. "This way."

Her shout woke Dork with a start. Then he saw the gribblers chasing the Charmseekers.

"Wait for me!" he cried and raced after everyone.

It was dusk and the light was growing dimmer by the minute. Sesame glanced at her watch.

"Two stars red. Only three to go!" she told Maddy, Gemma and Liz. She sounded exasperated. "This is all we need. Hardly any time to look for the charms and a bunch of gribblers on our trail!"

The girls could hear the gribblers crashing along behind. They didn't know it, but at dusk gribblers' eyesight is poor, because their eyes can't adjust to the change of light. Varg, Gorz and Bod were blundering into the supersize plants, which grew in this part of the jungle. Nevertheless, they could still hear and *smell* the Outworlders perfectly well.

"We're getting close," said Varg. "I got a good whiff of them jush NOW—

OW-OW-OW-OW-OW!"

The blood-curdling yell stopped the girls in their tracks. They turned and saw the biggest gribbler trapped by a grotesque-looking plant with leaves like

jaws. One of them
had snapped shut on
his foot and was dangling him
upside down. His companions
didn't appear to be much help.

"It's a snatchwort!" cried Bod excitedly.
"A blooming great snatchwort," agreed Gorz.
"I don't care what it is," moaned Varg.

"GET ME DOWN!"

The Charmseekers hurried away and left them to it.

"I hope *we* don't get stuck in one of those," said Maddy. "No wonder Pogg warned us about them!"

Meanwhile, Dork had been making good progress, and the gribblers' unfortunate encounter with the snatchwort had enabled him to catch them up. In the fading light, Varg, Gorz and Bod didn't notice him overtake them – and now Dork was gaining on the girls.

Sesame was frustrated at not yet finding a charm.

"Thank goodness we've left those gribblers behind," she panted, as she paused to check her watch again. "Three stars red! We *must* find a charm, before we go. Keep searching. PLEASE!"

Keeping their eyes peeled for a glint of silver that might be a precious charm, they battled their way through a tangled mass of roots, in what they hoped was the right direction for the gate. Every now and then they heard the sound of snapping twigs and, thinking it was the gribblers hot on their heels again, they hurried on. It was exhausting in that steamy place, and soon the girls felt tired. Suddenly Gemma got tangled in some kind of net.

"Help!" she cried. "I've caught my hair in something."

When Sesame, Maddy and Liz looked, they were horrified. Their friend was snared in an enormous spider web, slung like a hammock between two trees.

"Gross!" said Liz. "If that's the web, the spider
must be—"

"Wh-h-what s-p-p-pider?" gasped Gemma,
struggling to free herself.

"That one," chorused Sesame, Maddy and Liz.

Everyone screamed. A spider with eight very hairy
legs and bright, beady eyes was crawling over the
web. She (it was a female spider) wanted to see what
had been caught in her web.

Sesame knew what she must do.

"Hold it steady," she told Maddy and Liz. "I'm going to climb up there."

She scaled the sticky strands, ungluing her hands and feet as she went. It felt ghastly! Eventually she reached Gemma and managed to unhook her hair.

"Thanks!" said Gemma, and dropped to the ground.

Sesame felt the web sway. The spider was advancing . . .

"Get down, Ses!" cried Maddy.

"Now!" said Liz. "It's seen you."

But Sesame had spotted something, too. Caught in the web something glistened – something small and silvery, glinting in the pinkish starlight of Larissa.

It was the little butterfly charm!

Nine

The next few minutes were a blur with everything happening at once. Sesame remembered reaching out and clasping the silver butterfly – remembered holding it up for a moment, so they could all admire the exquisite little charm, glistening in the starlight.

Suddenly she felt the spider brush against her hand – but to her great surprise, Sesame didn't feel in the least bit threatened or squeamish. In that brief moment of contact, she knew the spider meant her no harm. It was a friendly gesture. Could it be the spider had been *protecting* the butterfly and recognised *her* as the one who should care for it? Sesame's thoughts were broken by voices – many voices – shouting.

"She's found a charm!"

"The butterfly!"

"Oh no, gribblers and—"

"STOP THIEF!"

The last voice was deeper than
the others. Sesame peered through
the web and was surprised to see
Dork, looking up at her from
below.

"Got you!" he said triumphantly.
"Give me that charm. You and your
friends are under arrest!"

"WHAT?" yelled Sesame and the
girls, in disbelief.
"You must be
joking!"

Dork made a grab for the charm. In that split
second, thoughts raced through Sesame's head. Dork
was one of the queen's officers. Didn't he remember
meeting her, the very first time she came to Karisma?
All the gatekeepers knew she was a Charmseeker, so
surely he must know too? Why did he think she was

a thief? Sesame was confused, but she was determined to protect the charm at all costs! She put the butterfly safely in her pocket and clambered out of the web.

Meanwhile Maddy, Gemma and Liz were arguing furiously with Dork.

Then came more shouts and the unmistakable stench of rotting fish; next thing Sesame saw were the gribblers wrestling with Dork!

"Quick!" she said to the others. "To the gate!"

The Charmseekers ran as fast as their legs would carry them. As they raced along, Sesame snatched another look at her watch.

"Four stars red . . ." she panted.

"Will we make it?" gasped Gemma.

"I hope so—" puffed Maddy.

"There's Pogg!" cried Liz.

Ahead of them they saw a hazy column of golden wings. The Golden Ringlets were waiting to take them home.

"Hurry, Charmseekers!" cried Pogg. "Hurry . . ."

And as the fifth star of Larissa glowed red, the girls ran through the gate and away with the butterflies, up into a starry sky.

Golden Ringlets

Can you find a pair of Golden Ringlets?
Only two of these butterflies have matching
wing patterns.

Much later that night, when Dork eventually returned to the palace, his uniform covered in cobweb, he recounted his side of the story in a letter to Queen Charm.

Your Majesty,

I wish to inform you that, acting upon reliable information, I attempted to arrest Sesame Brown and her friends, near Butterfly Bay.

I had been tracking the Outworlders through the jungle when, as luck would have it, I came across Sesame stuck in a spider web. I caught her in possession of one of your missing charms! I saw her holding the butterfly charm, with my very own eyes. But when I ordered Sesame to hand it over, she refused. Her exact words were, "You must be joking!"

Of course, I tried to take it from her, but I was overpowered by three foul-smelling gribblers. These doofers* thought I had retrieved the charm, and were determined to rob me. I therefore regret to inform Your Majesty that while wrestling with the gribblers, Sesame and her gang got away.

* *

Doofers – idiots of the first order, brainless

60

I would have given chase, but somehow the hairy spider tangled us up in its web and it took me ages to escape.

I am very sorry I failed in my duty, but I tried my best.

Your most trusted officer,

Dork

P.S. Here is Pogg's message. I'm sorry it's a bit crumpled. It's been in my pocket for a while.

Dear Queen Charm

I am pleased to report that the following Charmseekers have arrived at my gate!

Sesame Brown

Maddy Webb

Gemma Green

Liz Robinson

Yours sincerely

Pogg

Gatekeeper Five
Butterfly Bay

"Hurry now girls," Mrs Wilks was saying. "Everyone outside to see the butterfly garden."

Sesame, Maddy, Gemma and Liz had landed inside the butterfly exhibition at the Natural History Museum, just as the rest of their class were leaving. The four girls trooped out of the tropical butterfly house, in a daze.

"Come along, slowcoaches!" Mrs Wilks chivvied them. "We haven't got all day. There's much more to see before we go."

"It's SO weird," Gemma whispered to the others. "I don't think Mrs Wilks noticed we were missing. It's as if we've been here all the time!"

There wasn't another opportunity during the school outing for the girls to talk about their exciting adventure in Karisma.

"Let's have a sleepover soon," said Sesame, when they were parting at the school gates later that afternoon. "A secret Charmseekers sleepover!"

They all agreed it was a brilliant idea, and started

making plans, until Lossy arrived and took Sesame home.

As Sesame was unpacking her schoolbag, she remembered her lunch box. She'd left it in Karisma! Unfortunately, Lossy noticed it was missing too.

"Where's your lunch box?" she asked.

"I gave it to a dinosaur," said Sesame innocently.

"A likely story!" said Lossy. But she supposed Sesame had left it on the coach, and said no more.

Upstairs in her room, Sesame opened her jewellery box and placed the beautiful butterfly charm inside. Now there were five – the heart, the horseshoe, the shell, the cat and the butterfly. It was the first opportunity she'd had to look at the butterfly properly, since finding it in the spider web. The lovely pattern on its wings reminded her of the butterflies they'd seen at Butterfly Bay. What did Pogg call them? Golden Ringlets, that was it!

She suddenly remembered the little book the gatekeeper had given her too, and took it out of her pocket.

"I can't wait to go back to Karisma!" said Sesame, as she closed the lid of her jewellery box and settled herself to read . . .

The Princess and the Butterfly

MANY MOONS AGO there lived a king and queen who longed for a child. Years passed, until one day the queen gave birth to a daughter. The royal parents were delighted, but they couldn't decide on a name. For days and months they argued, quibbled and quarrelled, but still they could not agree! And, as time went by, their daughter became known as Princess No-name.

One morning, when the princess was eight years old, she woke with a terrible fever. The very best doctors came and went, prescribing pills and potions. Nothing they prescribed could make her better. The princess grew so ill, her parents feared she would die. In desperation, the king offered a reward for anyone who could cure Princess No-name.

One day a wise fairy called Sarm came to the palace, and told the king she knew of only one cure.

"The princess must sip nectar from the flower of a four-leafed clover," she said. "Nothing else will do."

On hearing this, the king and queen looked sad. Four-leafed clovers were rare; they were almost impossible to find! But Sarm promised to return soon with the precious nectar.

Sarm flew to the jungle, where Golden Ringlets were gathering in great numbers. It was the time of year when hundreds of these delicate butterflies migrated north,

to feed on the sweet, red clover. When Sarm
told the Golden Ringlets about the dying
princess, the butterflies agreed to help. They
rose together like a shimmering cloud, and
swarmed away.

The warm summer winds carried them
swiftly over the mountains and forests. Soon
the butterflies were flitting happily from
one sweet-smelling bloom to another,
pollinating the flowers and sipping
nectar, each one hoping to find a
stem with four leaves.

Among them was an old butterfly
called Floritta. She had migrated
many times before, and knew this
would probably be her last time.
Nevertheless her eyes were sharp
and, before long, she'd spotted a
four-leafed clover! Floritta sipped the nectar
through her proboscis like a straw, and
stored the precious liquid in her sac.

She would have liked to rest, but she knew she must return at once if Princess No-name was to be saved. So she plucked the lucky cloverleaf for the princess, and began the long journey home.

It seemed everything was against her. Flying over a mountain, a sudden storm blew up. Floritta was buffeted about in the wind and rain, and she found herself in an unfamiliar part of the jungle. She snagged her fragile wings on a thorn bush then she flew into the web of a hairy spider. Floritta struggled to unglue her legs from the sticky web, but the spider made it clear she meant her no harm.

"Rest," said the spider. "I will protect you."

Sometime later Sarm spotted Floritta, settled in the web, her torn wings spread in the warmth of the late afternoon sunshine. The fairy was saddened to see the exhausted butterfly, and could see she had also injured one of her legs.

"Take this," said Floritta feebly. She poured nectar into a tiny thimble, which Sarm had brought, and gave her the cloverleaf, too.

"Thank you," said Sarm. "I shall tell everyone of your bravery. You shall never be forgotten!"

Floritta sighed contentedly, then folded her golden wings and died peacefully in the setting sun.

Wiping tears from her eyes, Sarm flew as fast as she could to the palace. She found the king and queen by their daughter's bedside, weary from worry. Each held their breath as the princess sipped the nectar... and within the hour the fever had subsided. Soon Princess No-name was out of bed and wondering what all the fuss was about! Everyone in the palace cheered, and the heralds blew a fanfare to celebrate.

"You shall have your reward," the king told Sarm.

"No," said Sarm. "I don't deserve it. A butterfly called Floritta found the nectar. Floritta is the one who should be remembered."

"Floritta!" cried the princess. "I should love to be called Floritta. It's time I had a proper name!"

The king and queen agreed – it was the perfect name for their daughter. Ever since that day, Princess Floritta never tired of telling people about the brave little butterfly who'd saved her life. As for that four-leafed clover . . . the princess put it in a silver locket and wore it – just for luck!

Ten

The Silversmith smiles, as she sees another magic candle flicker and go out.

"Good!" she says, and breathes a contented sigh. "Sesame has found another charm. It is the little butterfly."

Now eight candles remain burning, and the Silversmith hopes it will not be long before her Charmseeker returns. But what strange stories she's been hearing about Sesame from the palace. And what was that puzzling letter from Dork all about?

"I must see Charm, soon," says the Silversmith, "and find out what's going on."

Meanwhile there are rumours in the Dark Forest that gribblers are gathering in great numbers. Ah, but that is another story. It must be told another day!

My thanks to Alexandra Gaffikin of The Natural History Museum, London, for information and source material about the Amazing Butterflies exhibition.